ABDO Publishing Company is the exclusive school and library distributor of Rabbit Ears Books.

Library bound edition 2005.

Library of Congress Cataloging-in-Publication Data

Kessler, Brad.
  John Henry / written by Brad Kessler ; illustrated by Barry Jackson.
      p. cm.
  "Rabbit Ears books."
  Summary: Retells the life of the legendary African American hero who raced against a
steam drill to cut through a mountain.
  ISBN 1-59197-764-9
   1. John Henry (Legendary character)—Legends. [1. John Henry (Legendary
character)—Legends. 2. African Americans—Folklore. 3. Folklore—United States.] I.
Jackson, Barry (Barry E.), ill. II. Title.

PZ8.1.K48Jo 2004
398.2—dc22
[E]

                                                                  2004045797

All Rabbit Ears books are reinforced library binding
and manufactured in the United States of America.

John Henry

Written by BRAD KESSLER

Illustrated by BARRY JACKSON

RABBIT EARS BOOKS

Way back a good while ago, when the United States was still bustin' out of its baby shoes, there lived a man named John Henry.

Now ain't no history books gonna tell you about John Henry, 'cause he was just too plain big for them books. But when it comes right down to it, John Henry was the mightiest, doggone greatest nation builder this country's ever seen. Oh, sure, you had your Washingtons and your Jeffersons— but they were just presidents. You see, John Henry was a steel-drivin' man.

Now some folks think they know all about John Henry and his famous race with the steam drill. But most of them don't even know a steel stake from a beefsteak. See, I was around when John Henry was king of the railroad camps, and I remember him just as clear as the Kentucky moon on an August night.

So y'all listen up, 'cause I'm gonna tell you the guaranteed, gold plated, ninety-nine-point-nine percent truth about John Henry.

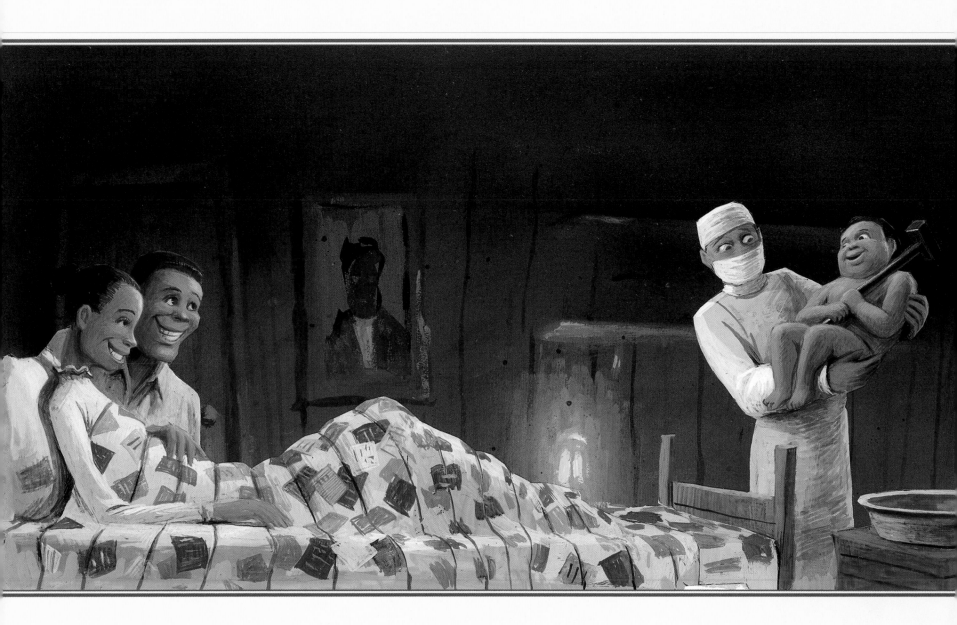

Now, it all started in a little village way down south in cotton country. Mama and Papa Henry were just your ordinary share croppin' folk, no different from the rest of us. They lived in a log cabin, and one springtime mornin', Mama Henry gave birth to a baby named John Henry.

Now folks knew right away there was somethin' different about John Henry. Shoot, ain't no ordinary baby born with a hammer in his hand! And ain't no ordinary baby weighs over forty-five pounds! But John Henry did.

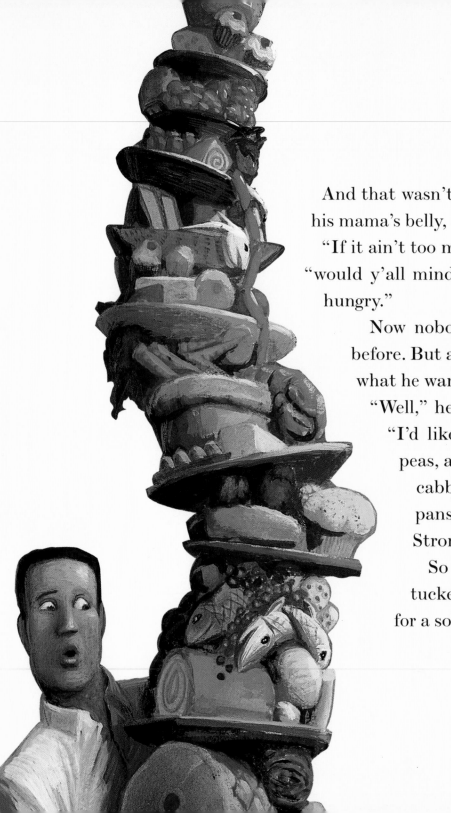

And that wasn't even the strange part. Not two hours out of his mama's belly, John Henry up and starts talkin'.

"If it ain't too much trouble," he said, just as sweet as sugar, "would y'all mind bringin' me somethin' to eat? I'm mighty hungry."

Now nobody ever heard a two-hour-old baby talkin' before. But after a while, Mama Henry asked John Henry what he wanted to eat.

"Well," he said, figurin' and calculatin' on his fingers, "I'd like eight ham bones, two pots of black-eyed peas, a three-foot slab of corn bread, three kettles of cabbage soup, a big heap of collard greens, four pans of peach cobbler, and two pots of coffee. Strong coffee. That is, if it ain't too much bother."

So John Henry ate pretty good. And he was so tuckered out when he was done, by jiminy, he slept for a solid week.

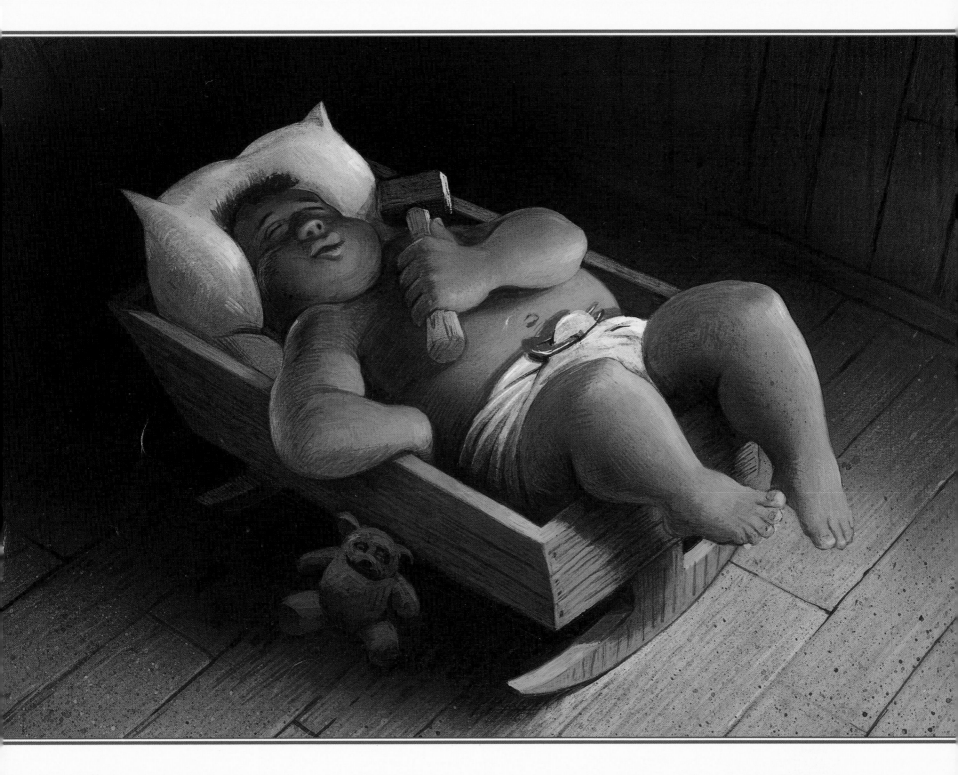

Well, the years went by and John Henry grew bigger. At two years old, he was jugglin' chickens for fun. At six, he was wrestlin' with razor-back hogs and jugglin' chickens at the same time. And at ten, why, at ten, John Henry was already a teenager.

But there was nothin' in the whole wide world that John Henry liked more than swingin' a hammer and singin' a song. He'd hammer hickory sticks, he'd hammer fence posts, cookin' pots, brass nails, boulders, anythin' he could get his hands on. He'd pound in the mornin', clang in the evenin'. His arms grew as solid as oak stumps, and his chest busted out bigger than a barrel.

Why, he grew so big that one day he couldn't even fit through the front door of his parents' cabin. And that's when John Henry decided it was time to leave home.

"Mama," he said one mornin', "I'm a man now. I'm a natural man, and I'm gonna find me a job with a hammer in my hand."

So John Henry left home and he walked north through the countryside. And as the sun went down at night, makin' the whole land light up like fire, he sang a song to himself:

"My name is John Henry and I'm a natural man.
I was born one morning with a hammer in my hand.
And if one day I find myself out all alone,
I'll hammer till the evening and pound my way back home."

One afternoon while he was walkin' in the lonesome woods, he stumbled across a road of iron rails. Those rails sparkled in the sunshine like silver, and beneath them were freshly cut wood ties, which smelled sweeter than a bag of balsam. And John Henry exclaimed, to no one in particular, "By jiminy, if this ain't a railroad track, then I'm an ox and a moron, both at the same time!"

Now John Henry, who was no ox and certainly no moron, was correct in his assessment. He had, in fact, stumbled onto the great Chesapeake and Ohio Railroad line, which was just bein' built around that time.

The C&O line, as people liked to call it, was goin' to connect up the eastern with the midwestern part of the United States. The railroad cut through some of the deepest, darkest, most howlin' wilderness of West Virginny, along hills and hollers, up mountains and down valleys, through woods as thick as a corn field in cuttin' time.

Well, John Henry knew right away he was onto somethin' big. And after a day of followin' those rails, he reached the top of a rise. And from that rise he saw where the tracks ended, far in the valley, and a whole assembly of men were livin' and workin'.

From up there, he could hear the clang and clink of hammers hittin' steel stakes, and to John Henry, it was the sound of heaven itself, a beautiful harmony of hammers ringin' over the hills like songbirds in early spring.

"Now that's a job for me!" John Henry yelled, beamin' from ear to ear. "A job for a natural man, who wants to build this land with a hammer in his hand!"

With that, John Henry scrambled down that rise as fast as his feet could take him.

When he got to camp, he was amazed. It was like nothin' he had ever seen before. There were men from all over the world workin' together with hammers! There were black men and brown men and red men; there were yellow men and white men, too.

So when John Henry got to camp, he just pushed his way straight ahead to the end of the line, picked up a nine-pound hammer and started drivin' steel stakes like it was goin' out of style. *Clang!* Hittin' here! *Bang!* Hittin' there! *Ding!* Hittin' this one! *Dang!* Hittin' that one!

Well after a while, everyone on that line stopped what they were doin' and started lookin' at this rather large, enthusiastic stranger. They saw right away that John Henry was just the naturalest man they had ever laid eyes on. Why he hammered those stakes so hard that smoke rose from them—and some of them even caught fire!

Soon the captain came over and started watchin' John Henry, too.

"Son," he said after a while, "you're the darn crackest steel-drivin' man I've ever seen. Name's Captain Tom, and I'd be honored if you'd work for me startin' tomorrow."

John Henry put down his hammer and smiled. "Pleased to meet you, Captain Tom. My whole life I've been waitin' to build this land with a hammer in my hand, and I don't aim on waitin' any longer. If it ain't any bother to y'all, I'm gonna start right now."

And with that John Henry set straight to work on the C&O Railroad.

Now drivin' steel ain't no Fourth of July picnic. Usually it takes a team of three men, all workin' in rhythm, to knock one stake into the ground. And usually there's a man called a shaker who has to hold the steel in place while it's bein' hit.

But John Henry had his own way of doin' things. First, he had the blacksmith build him two forty-pound hammers, which most men couldn't even lift. He'd hold one hammer in each hand like a pair of drumsticks. Then he'd take a steel stake, hurl it into the ground as if he were playin' darts, and smash it down with one hammer and then the next, *bing-bang-boom*, the whole time just singin' a hammer song. Fact is, John Henry couldn't really hammer without singin' and vice versa, 'cause for him, singin' and hammerin' were just different parts of the same thing.

> *"My name is John Henry. I'm a natural man.*
> *I was born one morning with a hammer in my hand.*
> *And if one day I find myself out all alone,*
> *I'll hammer till the evening and pound my way back home."*

Well, John Henry got so good at drivin' that steel he could do the work of ten men in half the time. He could hammer upside down, underarm, overarm, backhanded, blindfolded, sideways, front ways, and a few ways so complicated they can't even be explained without an acre of blackboards and a barrel of chalk. Heck, he'd work so fast that he needed his own waterman

just to keep his
hammers from catchin'
fire. ... steel ... could

... e, and he
... tton ball.
... he country,
... ver the
... ore line
... livin'
... or

Well, one day in late summer, when John Henry was back workin' the C&O line right around Big Bend Mountain, a stranger came into camp. Now, this stranger was all duded-up and dressed to the nines—a real city slicker who worked for none other than Cornelius Vanderbilt.

Now this fella brought with him a big contraption, which nobody had ever seen before. It was made of six kinds of steel, and covered with dials and gauges and drills and hammers.

"This machine is called a steam drill," the stranger explained when he got into camp. "And it can drive steel five times faster than any man."

Now this fella wasn't makin' no friends by sayin' a thing like that, 'cause nobody likes thinkin' a piece of metal can do his job. But them folks got to scratchin' their heads, lookin' over that machine, and figurin' that maybe—just maybe—it could. So them folks grew mighty quiet about the mouth. And just when things got so silent you could hear a ladybug yawn, John Henry stepped forward.

"I'll die with a hammer in my hand 'fore any

machine beats a man." He said it straight out, with no braggin' or sassin'. And then he went on: "A man's a man, and there ain't no machine that's better than a man. A man's got a heart inside, a big old beatin' heart. But a machine ain't got nothin' but a soul of cold steel."

On hearin' this, those folks nodded in agreement. But the stranger smiled, and there was a glint of gold in his eye.

"Does that mean you're willin' to compete with my steam drill to see who can drive more steel?" he asked.

"If that's what I got to do," John Henry said, "I'll do it. 'Cause I'm a natural man."

And so the contest was set for two days away at nine o'clock in the mornin': John Henry versus the steam drill.

And wouldn't you know it, two days later, just as the sun was stealin' up over Big Bend Mountain, folks came from all over the land, came streamin' into that valley. They came by foot, by horse, by buggy, and by locomotive train itself— just to see John Henry whup up on that steam drill.

At nine o'clock, the crowd fell silent and the official man shot his gun into the air. The contest had begun.

On the right side was the steam drill. And that steam drill straight away lurched into the lead, a-gurglin' and a-spoutin' and makin' metal racket to high heaven. There were a few fellas shovelin' pine knots in its belly for fuel, and that machine was drillin' holes into the ground just as fast as buckshot.

On the left side was John Henry, sweatin' and flexin' and lettin' loose with full John Henry force. *Clang!* Hittin' here! *Bang!* Hittin' there! The whole time singin' his song while his hammers kept the back beat.

So in this way, the hours went by. One hour. Two hours. Three, four, five hours. The sun climbed high up in the sky, then rolled back down. And John Henry's hammers got so hot, they were just glowin' like the sun itself. But that steam drill was still ahead.

At four o'clock that afternoon, John Henry and the steam drill were neck and neck. They reached the opening of Big Bend Tunnel, and went right inside. Folks waited outside where they could hear the contest goin' on. They heard the whine and screech of that steam drill, spittin' and screamin' like an alley cat. And over that awful sound, they could hear John Henry's voice, sweeter than the summer's corn, echoin' out of that tunnel.

> *"My name is John Henry. I'm a born*
>   *natural man.*
> *I was born in the morning with a hammer*
>   *in my hand.*
> *With these hammers and skill*
> *I can whip any steam drill."*

At five o'clock, just as the day was coolin' down, there was another gun shot, and the race had ended.

All was silent in Big Bend Tunnel. Outside, a hush came over the crowds, and that valley was as quiet as a juke joint on Sunday mornin'.

After a few minutes, the official man came walkin' out of the tunnel. He strode right down those tracks, held his hand up high, and yelled out:

"John Henry drove more steel than the steam drill. John Henry beat the machine!"

And hoo-boy, you shoulda heard that crowd explode into yippin' and yellin' and screamin', just as pleased as plum puddin' that John Henry had won. Folks was a-celebratin' and folks was a-dancin'.

Then John Henry came out of that tunnel, covered from head to toe in coal dust, coughin' and holdin' his gut as if somethin' had bust inside.

So the crowds hushed again, and John Henry laid himself on the ground.

"You have to forgive me folks," he said. "But I had to beat that steam drill, and I did. And now I'm goin' to my grave with a hammer in my hand."

Well, nobody could believe what they was hearin'. Why, John Henry just whupped that steam drill. But as he was layin' there, with his hammers crossed over his heart and his face covered in coal dust, John Henry up and died. Up and died right there, in front of all those folks, as the sun was goin' down for the night.

Now some folks say John Henry died of a broken heart 'cause he knew the steam drill one day would take the place of every steel-drivin' man in the land. Others say he died of breathin' too much coal dust.

Well, it turns out John Henry didn't really die at all. He just sort of went on a long, deep sleep from which he hasn't yet woken. And if you don't believe me, shoot, you can see for yourself.

Now, all you got to do is take a train, any train, out into the empty countryside. And in the evenin' or late at night, when the moon is big and fat and the wind is just right, you listen to the wheels chuggin' on the track, back and forth, back and forth, like the beat of a drum. And by jiminy, that's the sound of John Henry poundin' steel stakes to kingdom come. Yessiree, folks. That's the sound of John Henry, hammerin' his way back home.

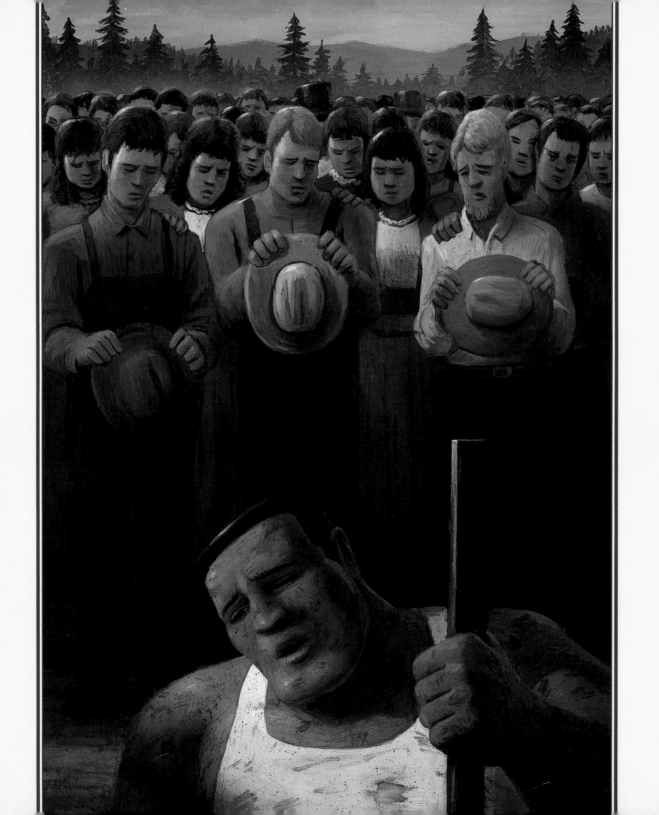